Hot Rod Hamster
AND THE AWESOME ATV Adventure!

By **Cynthia Lord**

Cover illustration by **Derek Anderson**

Interior illustrations by **Greg Paprocki**

Scholastic Press • New York

To Christopher and Lucas — C. L.

For Neal, Mae, and the whole Sturtz family — D. A.

LIBRARY OF CONGRESS CATALOGING-IN-PUBLICATION DATA
Lord, Cynthia.
Hot Rod Hamster and the awesome ATV adventure / by Cynthia Lord ; pictures based on the art of
Derek Anderson ; interior illustrations by Greg Paprocki. — First edition. pages cm
Summary: During their trail ride on all-terrain vehicles, Hot Rod Hamster and his friends stop to help Grandpa
Dog and two puppies, whose vehicle has tipped over and gotten stuck in the mud.
ISBN 978-0-545-76734-7 (hardcover : alk. paper) — ISBN 978-0-545-62680-4 (pbk. : alk. paper) [1. All terrain
vehicles — Fiction. 2. Hamsters — Fiction. 3. Dogs — Fiction. 4. Mice —
Fiction.] I. Anderson, Derek, 1969- illustrator. II. Paprocki, Greg,
illustrator. III. Title. PZ7.L87734Hou 2015 [E] — dc23 2014011739

10 9 8 7 6 5 4 3 2 1   15 16 17 18 19

Printed in Malaysia   108

First printing, January 2015

The display type was set in Ziggy ITC and Coop Black.
The text was set in Cochin Medium and Gill Sans Bold.
The interior art was created digitally by Greg Paprocki.
Art direction and book design by Marijka Kostiw

Hot Rod Hamster and his friends were out looking for adventure. The sun was shining. The day was fine. Hamster was delighted to see this sign:

AL's AWESOME ATV ADVENTURES!

Rent your ATV right next door. Bumps! Jumps! Down and dirty fun!

Three-wheeler.

Four-wheeler.

Track wheeler.

More wheeler.

Which would *you* choose?

Bridge trail. Tree trail.

Swamp trail. Sea trail.

Which would *you* choose?

Dog brings the map.
Hamster leads the way.
Mice ride behind.
What a happy day!

Dog picks up speed
as Hamster zooms uphill.
Mice hold on tight,
all ready for a thrill.

Dog makes a splash,
but Hamster hears a yelp.
All stop to listen.
Someone's yelling—

Push help?   Loop help?

Pry help?   Scoop help?

Which would *you* choose?

Hamster ties the rope.
Then he's on his way.
Mice hold their breath,
waiting for "Okay."

Dog hits the gas.
The wheels slip and slide.
Everybody cheers!
Such a muddy ride!